For my great-grandchildren, Caylin Nicole Johnson and Brandon Bailey Johnson.
For all the children in all the world, who, in order to grow healthily, need our love and poetry.
—M.A.

To Alexis, for her amazing peace.
—S.J. and L.F.

Read by the poet at the lighting of the National Christmas Tree,
Washington, D.C.
1 December 2005

Published by Schwartz & Wade Books
an imprint of Random House Children's Books
a division of Random House, Inc.
New York

Text copyright © 2005 by Maya Angelou
Illustrations copyright © 2008 by Steve Johnson and Lou Fancher

Visit us on the Web! www.randomhouse.com/kids

Educators and librarians, for a variety of teaching tools, visit us at
www.randomhouse.com/teachers

Library of Congress Cataloging-in-Publication Data
Angelou, Maya.
Amazing peace : a Christmas poem / Maya Angelou ; illustrated by Steve Johnson and Lou Fancher. — 1st ed.
p. cm.
ISBN 978-0-375-84150-7 — ISBN 978-0-375-94327-0 (lib. bdg.)
1. Christmas—Juvenile poetry. 2. Children's poetry, American. I. Johnson, Steve, ill. II. Fancher, Lou, ill. III. Title.
PS3551.N464A78 2008
811'.54—dc22
2007034327

The text of this book is set in Erasmus Medium.
The illustrations are rendered in oil, acrylic, and fabric on canvas.
Book design by Lou Fancher

PRINTED IN CHINA

10 9 8 7 6 5 4 3 2 1

First Edition

Amazing Peace

A CHRISTMAS POEM

BY

MAYA ANGELOU

PAINTINGS BY
STEVE JOHNSON AND LOU FANCHER

schwartz & wade books · new york

Thunder rumbles in the mountain passes
And lightning rattles the eaves of our houses.
Floodwaters await in our avenues.

Snow falls upon snow, falls upon snow to avalanche
Over unprotected villages.
The sky slips low and gray and threatening.

We question ourselves. What have we done to
    so affront nature?
We interrogate and worry God.
Are you there? Are you there, really?
Does the covenant you made with us still hold?

Into this climate of fear and apprehension,
    Christmas enters,
Streaming lights of joy, ringing bells of hope
And singing carols of forgiveness high up in the
    bright air.
The world is encouraged to come away from rancor,
Come the way of friendship.

It is the Glad Season.
Thunder ebbs to silence and lightning sleeps
    quietly in the corner.
Floodwaters recede into memory.
Snow becomes a yielding cushion to aid us
As we make our way to higher ground.

Hope is born again in the faces of children.
It rides on the shoulders of our aged as they
walk into their sunsets.

Hope spreads around the earth, brightening
all things,
Even hate, which crouches breeding in
dark corridors.

In our joy, we think we hear a whisper.
At first it is too soft. Then only half heard.

We listen carefully as it gathers strength.
We hear a sweetness.
The word is Peace.

It is loud now.
Louder than the explosion of bombs.

We tremble at the sound. We are thrilled
   by its presence.
It is what we have hungered for.
Not just the absence of war. But true Peace.
A harmony of spirit, a comfort of courtesies.
Security for our beloveds and their beloveds.

We clap hands and welcome the Peace of Christmas.

We beckon this good season to wait awhile with us.

We, Baptist and Buddhist, Methodist and Muslim, say come.

Peace.

Come and fill us and our world with
   your majesty.
We, the Jew and the Jainist, the Catholic and
   the Confucian,
Implore you to stay awhile with us
So we may learn by your shimmering light
How to look beyond complexion and
   see community.

It is Christmas time, a halting of hate time.

On this platform of peace, we can create
    a language
To translate ourselves to ourselves and to
    each other.

At this Holy Instant, we celebrate the Birth
  of Jesus Christ
Into the great religions of the world.
We jubilate the precious advent of trust.
We shout with glorious tongues the coming
  of hope.
All the earth's tribes loosen their voices
To celebrate the promise of Peace.

We, Angels and Mortals, Believers and
   Nonbelievers,
Look heavenward and speak the word aloud.
Peace. We look at our world and speak the
   word aloud.
Peace. We look at each other, then into ourselves,
And we say without shyness or apology or
   hesitation:

Peace, My Brother.
Peace, My Sister.
Peace, My Soul.